D1187872

Postman Pat
and the Greendale Ghost

Story by **John Cunliffe**
Pictures by **Joan Hickson**

From the original Television designs by **Ivor Wood**

André Deutsch/Hippo Books

Published simultaneously in hardback by
André Deutsch Limited
105-106 Great Russell Street, London WC1B 3LJ
and in paperback by Hippo Books, Scholastic Publications Limited,
10 Earlham Street, London WC2H 9RX in 1987

ISBN 0 233 98121 7 (hardback)
ISBN 0 590 70736 1 (paperback)

Made and printed in Belgium by Proost
Typeset in Plantin by Span Graphics, London

It was Hallowe'en.

Katy and Tom were busy.

They were making turnip lanterns.

And they were getting ready for the
Hallowe'en party.

Katy dressed up as a witch.

Tom dressed up as a ghost.

When Pat came with the letters, they jumped out on him.

Katy went, "Booooooooooooooooooo!"

Tom went, "Whoooooooooooo!"

Pat jumped. "Oh!"

Jess hid behind Pat and put his claws out.

Pat said, "I don't believe in ghosts."

"I do," said Mrs. Pottage, when she came out for her letters. "Don't you know the story of the Old Mill House?"

"Oh, that old tale," said Pat.

"Ooooh, tell us, tell us," shouted Katy.

"There's an old man rides over the bridge," said Mrs. Pottage, "and he has no head. And lights have been seen in the ruined mill at midnight."

"Ooh!" said Katy and Tom.

"But it's been empty for years and years," said Pat, "and all the windows are boarded up."

"I bet you daren't go there in the dark," said Mrs. Pottage.

" 'Course I dare," said Pat. "I'm not scared."

When Pat called at the church, Miss Hubbard was helping the Reverend Timms to get the church ready for All Saints Day.

"Do you believe in ghosts?" said Pat.

"There's no such thing," said Miss
Hubbard.

"The Lord will care for us," said the
Reverend. "Have no fear."

Pat called at Thompson Ground.

"Do you believe in ghosts?" he asked
Dorothy Thompson.

"Well," she said, "my gran said she
saw the ghost of her old cat, once, in
the barn."

"The cat's aunt, more like," said Alf.
"She never wore her glasses."

At the school, the children were playing
Hallowe'en games. "Do you believe in
ghosts?" said Pat.
"Yes!" they all shouted.

Pat called on Granny Dryden.

"Do you believe in ghosts?" he said.

"Of course I do," she said, "but I'm not afraid of them."

When Pat saw Ted Glen, mending a
wall, he stopped for a chat.
"Do you believe in ghosts?" said Pat.
"Well," said Ted, "I'm not sure."

Pat told Ted the story of the Old Mill House.

"Tell you what," said Ted. "Let's go and have a look, tonight."

"Tonight?" said Pat.

"Yes," said Ted. "Why not? Come round for a cup of tea, and we'll go after 'Top of the Pops'."

"Well...all right," said Pat.

Jess went to Ted's with Pat.

"He's good at smelling things out," said Pat.

It was dark when Pat and Ted set out
along the road to the Old Mill House.
The trees made it still darker; and
spooky.
Pat didn't like it.
Jess liked it.
He thought he might catch a mouse in
the dark.
Ted was singing a song from 'Top of
the Pops'.

"Whoooooooooooooo!"

"What's that?" said Pat.

"Owls," said Ted.

Creak . . . crackle!

"What's that?" said Pat.

"You stepped on a twig," said Ted.

Now it was really dark.

They were close to the Old Mill House.

"I don't like it here," said Pat. "Let's go home. There's a good film on TV."

"Don't be soft," said Ted. "I want to see this ghost."

They were near the bridge now.

"That's where the headless man rides his horse," said Pat.

Clank! Clank! Whirr! Swish!

"It's him!" said Pat. "Oh, Ted, it's him!"

The noises came nearer.

Clank! Clank! Whirr! Swish!

"By heck!" said Ted.

Nearer still.

Clank! Clank! Whirr! Swish!

They saw a light shining.

"I'm off," said Pat.

"Hold on," said Ted.

A hat, then a face, then a person came into view.

It was not a headless rider,
It was Miss Hubbard on her bike.
She was riding home after choir practice.
Her old bike went *Clank! Clank! Whirr! Swish!*

"Good evening, Pat and Ted," she
called, as she rattled by.

"Evening, Miss Hubbard," said two
wobbly voices.

"It's getting late," said Pat. "We'd
better go home."

But they could not see Jess now, and
Ted said, "Let's just have a look
at this old mill."

It was a spooky place, ghosts or no
ghosts.
They crept up to the old walls.
All was quiet.

Then,

Aaaaaaaaaaaaaaaaaaaaaaaaa!

Pat ran.

Ted followed.

Pat fell over a log.

Ted fell over Pat.

They landed in the middle of a prickly
bush.

What a rumption!

"Help!" shouted Pat, thinking the ghost
had got him.

A light shone on them.

"Whatever are you doing?" said a voice.

It was Miss Hubbard. She had come back with her torch.

She helped them out of the bush.

"Thanks, Miss Hubbard," said Ted.

"We thought the ghost had got us."

"Ghost?" said Miss Hubbard. "Don't be silly. There's no such thing."
Pat saw a shape on the wall. "What's that, then?" he said.

Miss Hubbard shone her torch.

"It's only Jess," said Pat.

"But there are two cats," said Tom.

"I think Jess has met a girl friend," said
Miss Hubbard.

Pat smiled. "And that was the noise we heard. It was Jess singing to his sweetheart. What a din!"

"I'd rather have 'Top of the Pops'," said Ted.

"It's not a patch on the church choir," said Miss Hubbard. "And we've had enough of ghosts for one night. I think it's time we all went home."

So they did.